The Brave Balloon of Benjamin Buckley

The
BRAVE
BALLOON
of
Benjamin Buckley

Barbara Wersba

Drawings by Margot Tomes

New York   ATHENEUM   *1966*

The Brave Balloon of Benjamin Buckley

Once upon a time many years ago, an English township called Peaceful discovered The Balloon.

Save for a farmer named Watchful they might never have discovered it at all, for on this particular morning the citizens of Peaceful were in bed. The sun was well up in the sky—all the cocks had crowed and the cows mooed—but it was a custom in Peaceful to oversleep. The Town-Crier dozed on the village green, his hat over his eyes. The Candlemaker slept in the back of his shop while mice nibbled the tallow. The Tailor snored under six quilts,

while the Baker dreamed of cream puffs beside an empty oven. At the foot of the street the Constable lay flat on his back in the jail, and in the Town Hall the Justice slumbered over a pile of law books, his wig on the floor. Even the Mayor, who was responsible for all comings and goings, was in the middle of a four-poster bed with a nightcap covering his bald spot.

But Watchful the farmer was awake. For two hours he had been sitting on the roof of his barn watching an ominous spot in the sky. At first he had thought it was a bird. Then he had decided it was a small rain cloud. Finally

he had reasoned that it
must be some kind of
star or heavenly body
off course. But as the
thing drew closer, re-
vealing itself in the
shape of an enormous
top with blue and yellow
stripes, Watchful be-
came alarmed. In terror

he called his wife, who climbed up onto the
barn with him. As the object drifted over
their heads, they saw that it had a small
basket dangling beneath. There was someone
in the basket, holding a flag in one hand and
saluting with the other.

"What is it?" cried Watchful's wife.

"A moon monster," said Watchful.

"Run," she screamed. "Tell the Mayor. It's

heading for town." Watchful ran. Through thickets and pastures and hillocks and copses. He woke the Mayor and he woke the Constable. He woke the Justice and he woke the Town Crier, who put on his hat and ran through the streets crying, "Moon mon-

ster," and "All men to the Square."

The Baker armed himself with a wooden spoon. The Tailor grabbed his longest needle. The Candlemaker brought a bag of candles to set the monster afire, and all

the ladies of the town brought brooms. Soon
the entire citizenry was assembled in the
Square, clad only in their night clothes.

The object was directly above them now,
and the person in the basket was waving his
flag heartily. A roar of anger and fear went
up from the crowd and they began to throw
things—teakettles and old shoes, cobblestones
and dictionaries. But before they could do any
damage, the blue and yellow top shuddered,
caved in, and sank to the ground dragging a

little anchor behind it. Immediately, the townspeople fell upon the monster with brooms and needles and knives. Its passenger, who was dressed in a helmet and checked trousers, might have been fatally injured save for a cry that rose from the back of the crowd.

"Stop! This is an airship, not a monster!"

All eyes were focused upon the bearer of this news, who turned out to be an intelligent child named Benjamin Samuel Joshua Tobias Buckley.

"The lad is correct," said the man in the checked trousers, who was extremely ruffled. "I seem to have developed a leak."

There was a murmur of surprise from the crowd.

"My credentials," announced the stranger, handing a scroll of parchment and ribbons to the Mayor.

"This will introduce," the Mayor read aloud, "Sir Christopher Crumble, Master Balloonist, who is travelling in his balloon *Surprise* in an attempt to cross the English Channel. He is a gentleman and a scientist. Kindly afford him every hospitality and do no injury to his balloon. He travels in the name of Progress and Imagination.

(signed)

The Balloon Society Of Tunbridge Wells"

"We all congratulate you," said the Mayor. "But pray, sir—what is a balloon?"

"Have you never heard of Ballooning?" Sir Christopher asked. "Balloonists? Balloono-philes? Ballooniana?"

"Alas, no," said the Mayor. "We are a

remote township."

"My dear sir," said Sir Christopher, stepping over to his vehicle, "This is a balloon. It is fast, progressive, and capable of air travel. It is borne aloft by means of certain lighter-than-air gasses which enable it to roam the heavens freely. It is a joyous vehicle, and I am astonished that you are ignorant of its existence."

The Mayor sighed. "You do us great honor by landing here. Allow us to give you a banquet."

"But of course," said Sir Christopher.

And that is how the word *balloon* came into the vocabulary of the township of Peaceful. Within a few hours the citizens were using such expressions as *light as a balloon, fast as a balloon* and *round as a balloon.* The Schoolmaster printed the new word on his blackboard and made pupils memorize it. In haste, the Mayor had a banner strung across town which read, PEACEFUL WELCOMES THE BALLOON, and the town's newspaper bore the headlines, BALLOON DISCOVERY IN PEACEFUL.

Now of all the inhabitants of Peaceful, the

person most excited about the arrival of the balloon was Benjamin Buckley. This child had spent his lifetime attempting to fly, a fact which grieved his mother considerably.

At the age of five Benjamin Buckley had shut his eyes and jumped off the tool shed, holding a parasol. Instead of flying to the moon, he had fallen into a cabbage patch, escaping with minor bruises. Two years later he had made wings from the feathers of three hundred chickens and leaped joyfully from the roof of the school house, receiving a sore ankle and instructions from

the Schoolmaster to write MEN ARE NOT BIRDS
fifty times. It was Benjamin Buckley's secret
desire to fly around the world, but he had
never found a vehicle for such a project. Thus,
the appearance of the balloonist made his
heart pound faster, and with new dreams of
voyages and stars he marched off to the
banquet.

Preparations for the festivities had been
hasty and elaborate. The town, embarrassed
at being ignorant of such a well-known thing
as a balloon, made up for this by showing Sir
Christopher every hospitality. The Mayor
proclaimed "Balloon Week." The Constable

gave all the prisoners in the jail a holiday. The Justice invented a new law on the legality of air travel, and the Tailor decorated the Town Hall with blue and yellow ribbons.

That evening, after a banquet of partridge, muffins, mince pie and ale, Sir Christopher mounted the rostrum in the Town Hall to address the citizens of Peaceful.

"I am angry and sad," he began. "Sad and angry. Yet sadder than angry—depressed."

"He speaks in riddles," whispered the Mayor to the Justice.

"He is a scientist," said the Justice.

"Oh," said the Mayor.

"How can it be," continued Sir Christopher, "that this township has no balloon? You have Millers, have you not? Weavers? Apothecaries? Village Idiots and Scholars? Justices and Poets? Yet among you there is not a single Balloonist, to say nothing of a balloon. For shame, gentlemen. You are behind the times. A Balloon Revolution has swept England while you slept. The entire country has become air-borne while you remained on the ground. The heavens are studded with balloons—drifting, travelling, racing, going up and down, backwards and forwards, to and fro—while you my friends, stay in one spot. Build a balloon, gentlemen, and quickly, lest history record you as a backward township of no imagination."

"Will history record us thus?" asked the Mayor.

"It will," replied Sir Christopher, "and worse."

"What use is a balloon?" asked the Constable.

"What use?" roared Sir Christopher. "You might as well ask what use the wheel is, or the teakettle. What use are Poetry and Science, Advancement and Progress? My dear Constable, I weep for your ignorance. In the cities there are plans for taxi-balloons and balloon sedans to transport gentlemen to work. Parcel deliveries will some day be made by balloon, and letters will be carried by a new system called 'air-mail.' There have been weddings in balloons and firework displays from balloons, balloon sailboats and military balloons. Horses have gone up in balloons as well as royalty. Famous actresses have thrown kisses from balloons. Clowns and acrobats have parachuted from ballons, and a certain gentleman I know has decided to live in one, though I have not heard from him recently. In short, my friends, history will not wait for you. Peaceful must enter The Balloon Age."

There was a shout of approval from the crowd. Then, quite forgetting himself, Benjamin Buckley jumped to his feet.

"I move that we build a Peaceful Balloon at

once," he said, "and that we engage Sir Christopher as Balloonist In Residence."

"Hear, hear," cried the grownups. "Hurrah!" echoed the children.

And the motion was passed.

From that time on the citizens of Peaceful spoke of nothing but The Balloon. Ladies' fashions were influenced by it, their hats and dresses taking on alarming shapes. The Schoolmaster introduced a new course into the curriculum of Reading, Writing, and Arithmetic which was called Aerostatics. The Town Poet wrote "Odes to Balloons," and the Concertmaster composed a "Balloon Oratorio for Three Voices." Meanwhile, Sir Christopher gave daily lectures on Ballooning, all of which were attended by Benjamin Buckley, who took voluminous notes.

"SILK," cried Sir Christopher, and without a murmur the ladies of Peaceful donated all their silk dresses for the balloon's envelope. "A wicker basket," he shouted, and the Town Weaver began to weave night and day. "Hydrogen," barked Sir Christopher at the Apothecary, causing this little man to tremble and consult a manual on Gasses. "Ballast," demanded Sir Christopher. "Statoscope. Charts and compass. A valve-line and a ripping panel. Drip-flaps and a trail-rope. A grapnel and a bottle of brandy for cold nights. A flag bearing an emblem, one striped sun-umbrella, and a small pistol for self-defense. Hurry gentlemen—history is waiting."

In the hills shepherds piped of balloons, and in the town children went to sleep at night with the word *balloon* upon their lips. But in the heart of Benjamin Buckley there was discontent. After the banquet he had rushed to Sir Christopher and volunteered to act as First Mate on the balloon's maiden voyage. Sir Christopher regretfully declined. Two weeks later, Benjamin applied for the position of Cabin Boy, Navigator, or Cook. Sir Christopher declined again, stating firmly that Ballooning was a man's job, not a boy's. This was a blow to Benjamin's pride, though a plan was taking shape in his mind that he thought might surprise everyone.

And then—one momentous day—the balloon was finished, a brightly colored envelope of stripes and checks, rosebuds and polka-dots. It had a trim basket, sturdy ropes, and an anchor made of brass. There had been some discussion about what to name it, such names as *The Gay Adventurer* or *The Heavenly Balloon Of The Township Of Peaceful* being offered. But finally the Mayor had decided simply to call it *The Brave Balloon,* and the citizens agreed.

The morning of *The Brave Balloon's* launching was fine and clear, with a strong breeze rippling the fields. Sir Christopher had been up since dawn, testing wind currents, tightening the rigging, and filling bags with ballast. *The Brave Balloon* stood in the middle of the Square, fastened by ropes and

tossed a little by the wind. All the townspeople had assembled and high upon a platform sat the Mayor, the Constable, and the Justice, in formal dress. Sir Christopher, who was again wearing his helmet and checked trousers, bowed and nodded after every speech. Then the Town Poet read a poem called "O Beautiful upon The Air" and the local chorus sang the "Balloon Oratorio for Three Voices."

The time for launching had arrived. Solemnly, Sir Christopher shook hands with the Mayor, the Constable, and the Justice, and ordered the ground crew to loose the outer bags of ballast. Free of this weight, the balloon struggled upward a few feet, secured only by the crew who were holding the outer ropes.

"My friends," said Sir Christopher, "this is surely a joyous occasion. Joyous and solemn. Yet more solemn than joyous. . ."

He did not finish. In a sudden burst of wind, *The Brave Balloon*'s ropes were tugged from the ground crew, causing them to lose their grasp and topple backward. Instantly the balloon rose into the air; and in the moment that it rose, two heads appeared over the side of the basket. One was the head of Benjamin Buckley and the other belonged to William, his cat.

Panic overcame the crowd. Some people fell to the ground in alarm, while others began to run after the balloon crying, "History" and "Come back." Sir Christopher stood dumb-struck, while beside him the Mayor fainted

dead away.
The Constable
ran to the bel-
fry of the Town
Hall and began
to toll a distress
signal on the great iron bell, but it was too
late. The balloon was air-borne, and amidst
the tumult and confusion a single voice could
be heard above the others. It was that of
Benjamin Buckley crying, "Farewell!"

Barns and houses and meadows dropped away as *The Brave Balloon* flew higher, and soon the town of Peaceful was left behind like a toy village scattered on the grass. Benjamin caught his breath as the countryside spread before him, dotted with miniature animals and farms. The sensation of flying was more beautiful than he had ever imagined, for the balloon seemed to be poised in space while hills and valleys rolled past beneath it. As the balloon reached its equilibrium point and leveled off, all feeling of movement disappeared and Benjamin found himself caught up in the silent wonder of the sky.

Benjamin Buckley had only intended to stow away on the balloon. Now, since he had become its captain, he put out his flag, straightened his cap, and with a beating heart, assumed command. First he checked his ripping-line, valve-line, and neck-line. Next he looked at his drip-flap, trail-rope, and grapnel. He saw that the ballast bags were secure. He studied the barometer, statoscope, and compass. He peered through the telescope, read

the charts, and hung out the parachute to air, for it smelled a bit musty.

The balloon had a small locker of provisions and a shelf of books. There were also blankets, crockery, postage stamps, and a curious box with the name *Splosh* written on it. This seemed to be for miscellaneous items, such as fishing lines and clothespins.

The first three things Benjamin had learned from Sir Christopher's lectures were these: 1) You cannot steer a balloon. 2) You can make it go up by throwing sand-ballast overboard. 3) Or down by releasing gas from the envelope. Sometimes you can find an air current going in the right direction, but you are always dependent on the wind and may find yourself in China when you mean to visit Africa. This was exactly what Benjamin Buckley had in mind, but on the first day of his journey he had experiences of a different sort.

Travelling with a southerly wind he swooped over a farm, frightening a herd of cows and causing them to stampede. Within minutes this herd was joined by a second herd which became panicky, stampeded, and was then joined by a third. By the time Benjamin had passed, all the cows in the village were galloping down the main street, frightening elderly gentlemen and upsetting applecarts.

Drifting with a westerly breeze, Benjamin passed twelve young ladies who were on their way to a Maypole celebration, their arms laden with roses. Upon seeing Benjamin they quite lost their heads and threw all their roses to him, though of course he could not catch them. By the time he had floated out of sight, the twelve young ladies were in tears and up to their ankles in rose petals.

Travelling to the
north, Benjamin passed
a castle where a gen-
tleman leaned out of a
tower, shot an arrow
at him, missed, and cried,
"Down with The Bal-
loon." This was quite
baffling to Benjamin.
As the balloon

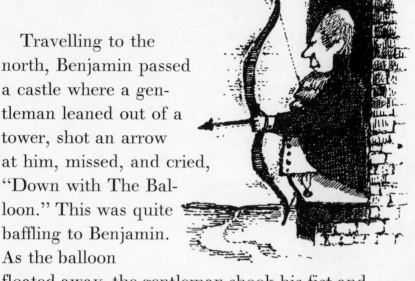

floated away, the gentleman shook his fist and
shouted something about The Empire.

In the east he came to a harbor where a
fleet of warships was anchored. Mistaking
Benjamin for a dignitary on official business,
the ships all raised their flags and gave him a
twenty-one gun salute with the sailors stand-
ing at attention. Not wishing to be discourte-
ous, Benjamin waved his own flag and bowed
politely to the Admiral.

The first night of *The Brave Balloon's*
journey was clear and warm. Benjamin gazed
at the heavens in awe as the balloon sailed
past stars and bobbed beneath a crescent

moon. The air was sweet, with a faint smell of roses, and the only sound was the gentle creaking of the rigging. A star fell through darkness, leaving a bright trail in its wake. Somewhere in a forest an owl hooted and was still. Benjamin lit a small lamp and prepared a supper of biscuits and toffee. Then, his dream of air travel come true at last, he drew his cat close to him, curled under a blanket, and went to sleep.

As the first rays of the sun lit the sky, Benjamin woke to find a sea gull staring at him. Leaping to the side of the basket, he saw that they were over the ocean and that the coast of England was out of sight. Since this was a perfect opportunity to begin his trip around the world, he hoped he would continue in this direction and see America.

He had just dropped a fishing line over the side of the balloon when a ship appeared on the horizon. Benjamin put out his flag to identify himself and waved. Drifting closer, he saw that it was not a ship at all, but a large raft. There was a lady sitting on it in a wicker

chair, knitting, and
beside her was a bird
cage with a canary
and quite a lot of lug-
gage.

"I say," she shouted,
waving to him, "could
you come down for
a minute? I need your help."

"Of course," shouted Benjamin, supposing
the lady to be shipwrecked, and releasing some
gas from the balloon he descended and tossed
her a rope.

"How do you do?" she said. "I am Miss
Blodgett, the first woman to cross the Atlantic
by raft."

"How do you do?" said Benjamin, tipping his cap. "I am Benjamin Buckley, Balloonist."

"I wonder if I might ask your help? You see, I've done a frightfully stupid thing—I've forgotten my sail."

"How did that happen?" Benjamin asked in surprise.

"I'm not sure," said Miss Blodgett. "Except that in the haste of departure, with so much luggage, and the bird cage to carry, I neglected to pack the one thing I really needed, which was my sail. I'm afraid I'll have to abandon ship and begin over again. There's no use in sailing without a sail. Don't you agree?"

"I do," said Benjamin, and in a gentlemanly fashion he dropped a rope ladder over the side of the balloon and helped Miss Blodgett aboard. Though quite stout, she climbed up nimbly.

"Where are you headed?" she inquired.

"America," Benjamin replied.

"I see," she said thoughtfully. "I myself am going to East Africa, but that's not at all in the same direction, is it? Do you suppose you could take me back to England? I'm sorry to be such a bother."

"No bother at all," said Benjamin, though privately he was a bit distressed by the delay.

Luckily, they soon found an air current going in the right direction and began to chat over tea and biscuits while Benjamin's cat eyed Miss Blodgett's canary.

"Balloons," mused Miss Blodgett. "Pretty things, but not practical. Why don't you travel by raft? Bigger and better rafts are being built every day. To the sea, my lad! Porpoises. Pirates. The foamy shores of Zanzibar! I say—when do you think we'll be home? There is another Englishwoman by the name of Margery Queep who also intends to cross the Atlantic by raft and I'm desperate to get a head start on her."

"We are home now," said Benjamin, pointing to the coastline in the distance.

"Fine," said Miss Blodgett. "You can let me off anywhere you please. I'll just hike back and build myself another raft."

Skilfully, Benjamin
brought the balloon
down over a forest and
anchored in an oak
tree. He helped Miss
Blodgett and her canary
down the rope ladder.

"You're a brave lad,"
she said. "What was
your name again?"

"Benjamin Buckley," called Benjamin as the
balloon began to rise. "Good luck in Zanzibar!"

As the spring winds carried *The Brave
Balloon* across England, the citizens of Peaceful went into mourning for Benjamin Buckley
—certain that he had either drowned in the
sea or gone to the moon. The word *balloon*
was banished from the town's vocabulary,
and in sorrow, people returned to their old
ways. The Justice cancelled his law on the
legality of air travel. Ladies' fashions returned
to normal. The Concertmaster destroyed his
"Balloon Oratorio For Three Voices" and the

Town Poet ceased to write "Odes To Balloons", preferring daffodils instead. The Mayor announced that the loss of Benjamin Buckley was Peaceful's first tragedy, and he ordered that a monument be erected in the Town Square. It was made of marble, and at its base were the words:

IN HONOR OF
BENJAMIN BUCKLEY
LOST IN A BALLOON
SOMEWHERE ABOVE ENGLAND
IN THE SPRINGTIME

Benjamin Buckley, of course, was not lost at all. At the very moment when the monument was being erected to him, he was anchored above a meadow in Shropshire, eating blackberries. *The Brave Balloon* had been through three thunderstorms and one minor hurricane—William had almost fallen out of the basket in the excitement—and all of the biscuits were waterlogged. While Benjamin had found himself perfectly able to cope with these adventures, the envelope of his balloon was now drooping sadly due to a lack of gas. As he sat there wondering how to proceed, a voice said,

"Good morning."

"Good morning," replied Benjamin, looking around for the owner of the voice.

"Over here," it said, and Benjamin saw a gentleman in tweeds sitting on top of a tree.

"I see you are up for an outing," said the gentleman. "Or should I say, out for an upping?"

"Not exactly," said Benjamin. "Who are you?"

"I am a Birdwatcher," he replied, "And I have already seen three chaffinches, a thrush, and a tiny wren."

"Why do you watch birds?"

"Because it thrills me. Why do *you* sit in a balloon?"

"For the same reason."

"Nonsense," the gentleman replied. "Balloons are decidely unthrilling. Also unnatural, unesthetic, and unnice. Where do you think you're going in that one?"

"Around the world," said Benjamin. "Borneo, Tripoli, Madagascar, and Siam."

"Absurd!" cried the gentleman. "How dare you disturb international relations that way? Do you want to start a war? Suppose the French see you! Balloons are highly capricious and drift wherever they please."

"That's exactly why I like them," said Benjamin pleasantly.

"Do you know where I could get some gas?"

"I may and I may not," said the Bird-watcher angrily. "Some of us, you know, are content to stay on English soil. While others seem to have nothing better to do than fly to 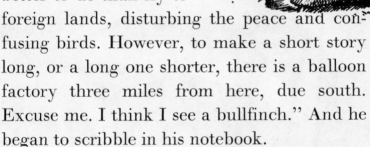 foreign lands, disturbing the peace and confusing birds. However, to make a short story long, or a long one shorter, there is a balloon factory three miles from here, due south. Excuse me. I think I see a bullfinch." And he began to scribble in his notebook.

With a smile and a wave at the foolish gentleman, Benjamin released some ballast and found an air current to the south. Within a half hour he saw an enormous pink building in the shape of a balloon. There were brightly colored flags flying from its turrets, and adjoining it was a parking area where balloons of all sizes were anchored.

Benjamin caught his anchor on a turret above the factory, climbed down the rope ladder, and was immediately surrounded by five men wearing white smocks.

"Very interesting," said the smallest and fattest man. "What model is it you have here?"

"This is *The Brave Balloon*, from Peaceful," said Benjamin.

"Oh," said the fat man, "I thought it might

be model 264-B. What a charming envelope.
So many colors. And a roomy basket. Ah, I
see you have a drip-flap. Very good. How has
your trail-rope been working? Never mind, I
suppose it works
quite well. Any

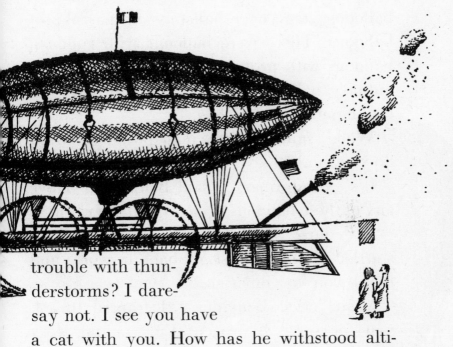

trouble with thun-
derstorms? I dare-
say not. I see you have
a cat with you. How has he withstood alti-
tudes? Never mind, never mind. Come and
see our factory."

Taking him by the arm, the little man and his assistants led Benjamin into the factory where dozens of men in white smocks were working on balloons. There were net-makers and basket-weavers, a silk department and a hydrogen laboratory, a rigging workshop and a drafting room for new designs. To his delight, Benjamin saw small balloons and tall balloons, stagecoach balloons and parcel-post balloons. There were balloons with rudders, balloons with propellers, a neat little fleet of military balloons, and one huge dirigible in the shape of a fish.

"Well," said the little man proudly, "what do you think?"

"It's extraordinary," said Benjamin. "Have any of these balloons been around the world?"

"Of course not," said the man, looking startled. "Now I must get back to work, and thank you for your visit."

"Wait!"cried Benjamin. "I wanted to ask you for some hydrogen. I'm running very low."

"Oh ho," said the fat man. "So that's what

you want? Hydrogen? Ah ha. And how do you intend to pay for it? Are you rich?"

"No," said Benjamin modestly. "But one day I shall be famous, and then I can repay you."

"What makes you think that?"

"My balloon," Benjamin replied. "It's a special balloon and very brave. I plan to take it to places where balloons have never been before. One day I shall see America from the sky, and fly past Greenland. I shall wave to people in Singapore, and visit lands that no one has discovered."

"Superb!" cried the little man. "I approve. Bring the hoses," he called to his assistants. "This lad needs gas."

The hydrogen hoses were brought to the roof, and within minutes the envelope of *The Brave Balloon* began to swell and expand and grow round again.

"*Bon voyage*," called the fat man. "Greet the Eskimos for me!"

With a full envelope of gas, *The Brave Balloon* travelled upward at a rapid pace. William perched on the rim of the basket, while once more Benjamin studied the charts and made ready for his voyage. Beneath him the fields of England glowed softly in the sunset. Cows were being led in from pasture. Wagons rolled lazily down country roads; and as Benjamin gazed at the horizon, he dreamed of other sunsets—on deserts and alps, canyons and oceans—sunsets over Spain and India and Egypt. The winds were promising, and when dusk had brought a cool light into the heavens, he went to sleep.

He woke the following morning to find himself not in Tripoli—or even France—but thoroughly becalmed. There was not a breath of air stirring and *The Brave Balloon* hung motionless in the sky. With a sigh of disappointment, Benjamin began to fix breakfast. It had rained during the night, and he was just mopping up some puddles when a voice at his elbow asked,

"Will you have a cup of tea?"

Benjamin looked around to find another balloon sitting alongside him in the air. Its basket was in the shape of an English cottage

with a thatched roof, and there were lace
curtains and flower boxes at all the windows.
A man sat on the veranda, sipping a cup of
tea and reading a newspaper.

"We seem to be becalmed," he said. "Nuis-
ance, isn't it?"

"Who are you?" asked Benjamin.

"Edward Queep," the man replied. "Husband of Margery Queep, the first woman to cross the Atlantic by raft."

"I thought that was Miss Blodgett," said Benjamin.

"Oh, no," replied Mr. Queep. "Bertha Blodgett's been having some trouble with her raft, I hear. My wife has started ahead of her. Aren't these calm days dreadful? I haven't made any progress all morning."

"What a fine balloon you have!"

"Isn't it?" said Mr. Queep. "I've been up for two years now, and it couldn't be more delightful. Mrs. Queep is involved in ocean travel; and since I hate the noise of the cities and the bustle of the towns, I've been living in the sky, so to speak."

"This is my maiden voyage," said Benjamin. "But I intend to see the world."

"How lovely," said Mr. Queep. "Do try to visit Arabia on the way. I have a dear friend there who is an Astronomer.

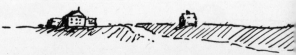

Have you seen any eagles this morning?"

"Beg pardon?"

"Eagles," said Mr. Queep, handing Benjamin a cup of tea. "Whenever I am becalmed, I look for passing eagles. I use them to transport me. Have you seen any?"

"I'm afraid not," replied Benjamin, wondering at the gentleman's sanity.

"Pity. There was a charming rainbow this morning. Did you watch it? O the pleasures of living in the air! Rosy clouds and drifting stars. Solitude. I don't think I'll ever go down again. Ho ho," he said suddenly, "I see an eagle."

There was indeed an eagle flying by, and soon it was joined by a second eagle. To Benjamin's amazement, Mr. Queep made a lasso of some twine and harnessed the birds as they passed.

"I'm off," he cried to Benjamin. "You may keep the teacup. Give my regards to the world!"

"I shall," called Benjamin waving his cap, and soon the cottage, the balloon, Mr. Queep, and the eagles were out of sight.

That evening a wind came from the south, and Benjamin and William found themselves flying swiftly over the countryside. A sprinkling of stars dotted the sky, and on the horizon an orange moon pulled itself over the treetops. For the first time in days, Benjamin felt that he was on his way. In honor of the occasion he put on his cap and hoisted the flag. But just as he had begun to determine his course by the compass, there was a deafening explosion. Its impact almost sent him hurtling out of the balloon and caused some of the provisions to slide overboard. His first thought was that the French had finally invaded England. He was about to man his battle station when there came a great burst of purple stars —and Benjamin realized that he was in the midst of a fireworks display.

The sky was filled with sprays of light, bursting and cascading to earth where thousands of people cheered. Some pink stars bounced into the balloon's basket and he rushed to stamp them out. Then a shower of blue stars drifted down and caught onto the rigging. Benjamin had just extinguished these when there was a burst of light brighter than any of the others. Looking up, he saw another balloon above him, on fire.

The woman in the balloon's basket was dressed in a spangled costume and she was running from side to side, uttering little cries of distress. She was quite pretty and had obviously gone up to release some fireworks. Now the envelope of her balloon was blazing brightly and she was descending at a rapid speed. With great calm, Benjamin tossed his rope ladder over the side and called to the woman to catch it as she passed. Nodding her head, she waited until her balloon was opposite his—then she jumped. She caught the rope ladder just in time and hung on, swaying bravely, as they drifted downward.

"Thanks for the ride," she called up to Benjamin. "My name is Margery Queep."

"I thought you were crossing the Atlantic," he shouted.

"Changed my mind," called Margery. "Decided to become a lady balloonist instead. Aren't balloons lovely? So much nicer than rafts. Do you know my husband?"

"I met him this morning," shouted Benjamin.

"And Sir Christopher Crumble?"

"My balloon instructor," called Benjamin.

"How jolly," cried Margery Queep. "What did you say your name was?"

"Benjamin Buckley."

"Benjamin Buckley!" she exclaimed. "Why, you're supposed to be dead. I read it in the *Manchester Balloon News* last Thursday. Good-bye now. I'm ready to jump."

As thousands watched in silence, Benjamin dipped *The Brave Balloon* over a rooftop and released Margery Queep, who landed in a box of flowerpots. There was a cheer from the crowd and thunderous applause. The King, who was sitting in a grandstand watching the event, turned to the Chancellor and asked,

"Who is that lad?"

"My goodness," said the Chancellor, "I don't know."

"Find him for me," ordered the King. "At once."

All the Chancellor could see of *The Brave Balloon* was a dot against the stars, and he wondered how he could find something in the air when he was on the ground. Nevertheless, he instructed the King's men to locate a boy in a balloon, and one hundred of them set out on horseback.

They galloped for two days and two nights with a General named Broome bringing up the rear in a small coach, and on the morning of the third day they found Benjamin Buckley drifting low above a field of buttercups.

"Greetings," cried General Broome, jumping from the coach, "and the compliments of the King. Now let us be off."

"Where to?" called Benjamin.

"To London," roared General Broome. "You're to go to see the King!"

"I'd be delighted," said Benjamin, who was astonished at the invitation. "Which way is London?"

"I'll tow you there," said the General. "Throw me a rope. There's a good lad."

Benjamin threw a rope over the side of the balloon, and General Broome tied it onto his coach. Then, with a fanfare of trumpets and

bugles, the soldiers, the coach, and *The Brave Balloon* proceeded towards London.

As they neared the city, General Broome unfastened the balloon and Benjamin soared upward. As he flew over the palace roof, he released some gas, anchored on a gargoyle, and climbed down the rope ladder. A courtier was waiting for him, and bowing, escorted him into the palace. Benjamin's heart beat nervously as they made their way down a long marble corridor. Gentlemen in powdered wigs bowed low. Ladies-in-waiting swept by with a

swish of silk. Then the massive doors of the
throne room swung open and Benjamin saw
the King.

On a dais of gold sat a very small man with
graying locks. He was sitting on the throne in
a depressed sort of way, leafing through pic-
ture books and eating toffee. But his eyes lit
up when he saw Benjamin and his cat.

"Oh good!" he said. "Are you the balloonist?"

"Yes sir," said Benjamin as he knelt.

"I'm happy to see you," said the King. "Sit
down, sit down. I want to ask you something."

Benjamin and William sat at the foot of the throne, and the King leaned forward.

"Young man," he said urgently, "I want to go up in a balloon and no one will let me. The Chancellor says it's too dangerous, the Queen is afraid I'll catch cold, the Prime Minister thinks I'll get lost, and the Chief of Protocol states that it's not proper. But I simply must go up in one. Will you take me?"

"Of course," said Benjamin. "Why do you let them bully you?"

"I don't know," said the King sadly. "But my life has grown weary to me and nothing seems lovely any more except balloons. I dream of balloons. When I look into my porridge bowl, I see them. When I gaze at the stars, I think of them. Everything round reminds me of them, everything bright, everything airy. If I could only have a balloon, I would be a happy King. When will you take me for a ride?"

"Now," said Benjamin firmly. "Follow me."

Slipping through a side door and up a secret passageway, they reached the palace roof and climbed aboard the balloon. After making the King comfortable and giving him a parachute, Benjamin released ballast and they shot up through the air and soared over the Thames.

"What a view!" cried the King. "How round and bright! How airy!"

Benjamin prepared lunch and pointed out sights of interest as they flew over London. The King was as excited as a child and kept clapping his hands and throwing his jewels overboard to see them fall to earth. He even tossed his crown over in the excitement and danced a jig as the wind carried it away.

"Good heavens," said the King, peering through Benjamin's telescope, "I think I see France! What a marvellous adventure. Do you do this every day?"

"Every day," said Benjamin happily. "I live up here."

"How glorious," sighed the King. "Look at that meadow! Ah, how beautiful the world is— I'd quite forgotten."

It was mentioned earlier that at the start of Benjamin Buckley's travels a man in a castle shot an arrow at him. This person's name was Sir Morris Mugby, and he hated balloons. Certain that all balloons were foreigners and enemies of The Empire, it was his habit to sit in the tower day and night with bow and arrow. Late that afternoon Benjamin and the King flew directly over Sir Morris' castle.

"Thundering thunderstorms," he cried, "it's the King—and in a balloon! Long live The Empire," he called uncertainly. "Up with The Balloon!"

The King did not hear him, for he was busy counting chimney tops and coaches. But soon after this, Sir Morris burned his bow and arrow and took to balloon travel himself, a wiser and calmer man.

It was with much sadness that the King parted from Benjamin Buckley that night. They had come down over a meadow, and the royal soldiers, who had followed, waited to take the little man back to the palace. As they stood under the stars with the cool grass swaying at their feet, the King took Benjamin's hand.

"This has been the happiest day of my life. I don't suppose you'd want to stay on and become Royal Balloonist? We could have lovely times together."

"I'm afraid I can't," said Benjamin gently. "You see, there are voyages I want to make. Somewhere there are stars I haven't seen yet, and oceans—great deserts, and sunsets on the other side of the world. England is beautiful, but there is a dream in me to go farther."

"I understand," said the King, "for I have had everything in life except the things I dreamed of. People have envied me, not knowing my loneliness. Now when I am lonely, I shall think of you and your balloon and your cat, sailing the skies; and in payment for this day, I shall give you a pension for the rest of your life. Perhaps that way you won't forget me."

"I shall never forget you," called Benjamin as *The Brave Balloon* drifted upward; and he waved at the King until the little man and his soldiers seemed like discarded toys under the moonlight.

Benjamin Buckley had been disturbed to hear that the citizens of Peaceful thought him dead, and he immediately set his course for home, landing there two days later. The Town Crier ran through the town announcing his arrival, children danced in the streets, and

brave men wept for joy at his return. The Mayor gave him the grandest banquet the town had ever seen; and Sir Christopher Crumble, who was now retired, decorated him with twenty silver medals. Poems were read in his honor, oratorios sung on his behalf, and the word *balloon* returned happily to Peaceful's vocabulary.

Benjamin was now very rich, but since he had never needed money, he gave most of the King's pension to the citizens of Peaceful, that they might have all the balloons they wanted. He also sent a sum to the balloon factory, purchased a town house for his mother, and bought presents for the friends he had made on his travels. He mailed an extra supply of sails to Bertha Blodgett and an enormous bird book to the Birdwatcher. To Edward Queep he gave an eagle harness of the finest leather, and to Margery Queep, a box of lavender rockets. He dispatched a manual on ballooning to Sir Morris Mugby, and with much love, sent the King a portfolio of balloon pictures in water color.

And then—no one could be sure exactly when it happened—Benjamin Buckley rose into the air and was not seen again. Some people said that he had taken a holiday, while others feared he was gone forever. Notices were posted in the *Manchester Balloon News*, and an anxious correspondence took place between the Queeps and Bertha Blodgett. But though they waited for him every day, and though the King sat by his window every night, *The Brave Balloon* did not return.

As weeks turned into months and months rolled into years, strange messages began to reach the shores of England. Sea captains off Tripoli reported a striped onion bouncing in the sky, and toreadors in Mexico complained

that an object made of rosebuds had frightened their bulls. Eskimos said that they had seen a flying igloo of polka dots, while American Indians announced that a young

moon-god had visited
their hunting grounds.
In the jungles of Af-
rica, natives made of-
ferings to a person
who seemed to be sit-
ting in the clouds with
a cat, and Australian
bushmen wrote of stam-
pedes among kanga-
roos. Fishermen in
Greenland, shepherds

in Greece, holy men in
Siam, all reported that
something strange and
beautiful had passed
over their countries.
From the north pole
to the south pole came
tales of an object travelling on the wind. It was
called an air-vehicle,
an onion, a sky-carriage,
an unidentified object,

a top, a flying radish, and an Arabian Astronomer even declared it to be a new star. It was
an odd kind of star, he said, for it appeared
over his country only once a year, shining
softly. Then it faded, leaving a lonely place
against the sky.

But the King, who sat by his window every
night watching the heavens, had not forgotten
the happiest day of his life. He knew that this
shining journey belonged to a boy, a cat, and
a very Brave Balloon.

GLOSSARY

Aerostatics	The science of lighter-than-air gasses.
Ballast	Something which gives added weight to the balloon and can be thrown overboard when the balloonist wishes to go higher: usually, bags of sand.
Ballooniana	Collected books, pictures, and documents on balloons.
Balloonophile	One who is especially fond of balloons.
Barometer	An instrument that records atmospheric pressure; used by balloonists to determine heights.
Basket	The car suspended beneath the balloon.
Drip-flap	A little awning on the envelope to keep rain and moisture off the crew.
Envelope	The balloon itself; made of silk and inflated with gas.
Equilibrium point	The point at which the balloon floats smoothly. Equilibrium is reached when the weight of the balloon equals the weight of the air around it.

Grapnel	The anchor.
Hydrogen	A lighter-than-air gas.
Neck-line	A cord that holds down the bottom of the envelope when it becomes flabby through loss of gas.
Ripping-line	A line leading to the *ripping-panel*: a small section of the envelope that can be torn out for quick deflation; good for emergency landings.
Splosh	Odds and ends.
Statoscope	An instrument to show the rate of fall or climb.
Trail-rope	A heavy rope, which at low altitudes trails on the ground and acts as automatic ballast.
Valve-line	A line leading up through the balloon to the *valve*: the opening which releases gas. The valve-line is pulled when the balloonist wishes to descend.